Little Princesses
The Dream-catcher Princess

www.kidsatrandomhouse.co.uk/littleprincesses

Little Princesses
The Dream-catcher Princess

By Katie Chase

Illustrated by Leighton Noyes

Red Fox

Special thanks to Sue Mongredien

THE DREAM-CATCHER PRINCESS
A RED FOX BOOK 9780099488354

First published in Great Britain by Red Fox,
an imprint of Random House Children's Books

This edition published 2006

3 5 7 9 10 8 6 4

Series created by Working Partners Ltd
Copyright © Working Partners Ltd, 2006
Illustrations copyright © Leighton Noyes, 2006
Cover illustration by Nila Aye

Set in 15/21pt Bembo Schoolbook

Red Fox Books are published by Random House Children's Books,
61–63 Uxbridge Road, London W5 5SA,
a division of The Random House Group Ltd

Addresses for Random House Group Ltd companies outside the UK
can be found at: www.randomhouse.co.uk

THE RANDOM HOUSE GROUP Limited Reg. No. 954009
www.**kids**at**randomhouse**.co.uk

The Random House Group Limited makes every effort to ensure that the
papers used in its books are made from trees that have been legally
sourced from well-managed and credibly certified forests. Our paper
procurement policy can be found at: www.randomhouse.co.uk/paper.htm.

Mixed Sources
Product group from well-managed
forests and other controlled sources
www.fsc.org Cert no. TT-COC-2139
© 1996 Forest Stewardship Council
FSC

A CIP catalogue record for this book is available from the British Library.

Printed and bound in Great Britain by
Cox & Wyman Ltd, Reading, Berkshire

Chapter One

Rosie Campbell stood at the entrance to the maze in the grounds of the castle and grinned at her younger brother. "Fancy a race?" she asked him.

Luke nodded eagerly. "Last one out the other side has to tidy the other's bedroom!"

Rosie laughed at the cheeky look on Luke's face. Her little brother was always looking for ways to get out of doing his chores. "Well, OK," she said teasingly, "if you're sure you want to tidy my bedroom . . . I mean, it is a bit of a mess . . ."

Luke smiled. "Not as messy as mine," he said cheerfully. "It's going to take you ages to tidy up all my dinosaurs!"

Rosie chuckled. "On your marks . . . get set . . . go!"

The two charged into the maze, Luke bearing off to the left and Rosie taking the right-hand path. They'd both been through the enormous hedge maze lots of times before, but neither of them knew the quickest way around it yet.

Rosie couldn't help grinning to herself when she heard Luke whooping with excitement as he ran. Luke just loved living here in Great-aunt Rosamund's castle. And so did Rosie! She still couldn't believe that her family had it all to themselves for a couple of years, while Great-aunt Rosamund was travelling the world.

Rosie slowed to a jog, remembering how excited she'd felt when she'd first read the message her great-aunt had left her, telling her to look out for little princesses around the castle. That very evening she'd found one, right there in her bedroom. And from then on she'd found princesses in all sorts of places, and had the most magical adventures with every one!

The sound of Luke's voice had faded into the distance and, as Rosie looked around, she realized that all she could see was the blue

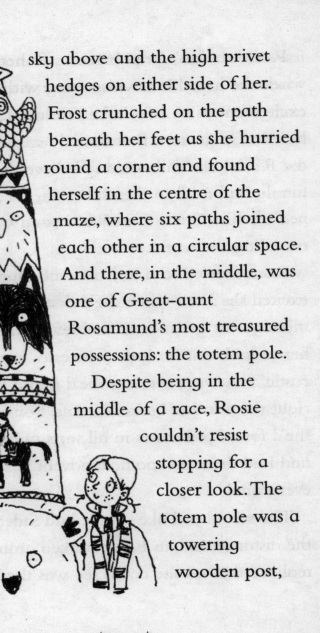

sky above and the high privet
hedges on either side of her.
Frost crunched on the path
beneath her feet as she hurried
round a corner and found
herself in the centre of the
maze, where six paths joined
each other in a circular space.
And there, in the middle, was
one of Great-aunt
Rosamund's most treasured
possessions: the totem pole.
Despite being in the
middle of a race, Rosie
couldn't resist
stopping for a
closer look. The
totem pole was a
towering
wooden post,

intricately carved and brightly painted in shades of black, red, white, turquoise, green and yellow. It was five times the height of Rosie and so thick that Rosie couldn't quite touch her own fingertips when she put her arms around it.

Great-aunt Rosamund had once told Rosie that her own father, Rosie's great-great-uncle, had brought it home from his travels. He'd been an explorer, and had lived with a tribe of Native American Indians for several years. The totem pole had been their parting gift.

Wow! thought Rosie, running her fingers over the weathered wood. She remembered her great-aunt telling her that the Native American Indians used totem poles as a way of recording stories. Every carving on the pole represented another part of the overall tale.

Rosie gazed at the carvings, wondering what the story of this particular pole was. There were many figures carved, one on top of the other, including an owl, an eagle, a star and a creature that looked like a playful dog. For the first time, Rosie noticed a carving of a girl on horseback. She looked closely at her. The girl was staring into the

distance with a determined look on her face and she wore a pretty beaded circlet around her head.

Rosie's heart quickened. "Could this be another little princess?" she wondered aloud. There was only one way to find out!

Rosie dropped into a curtsey. "Hello," she whispered to the girl on the horse.

The word had barely left her lips when a gust of wind swirled around Rosie, and she could suddenly smell the fresh, sharp tang of pine trees. A flurry of pine needles whirled dizzily around her, and Rosie was swept right off her feet. Another adventure was beginning!

Chapter Two

As quickly as it had picked up, the wind died, and Rosie found herself standing on firm ground once more. The sky overhead was the dark indigo blue of night and the cool air smelled of pine trees.

Rosie jumped as somebody suddenly grabbed her arm and dragged her to the ground. "Hey!" she gasped in surprise.

The full moon slid out from behind a cloud, looking like a shiny silver coin in the sky. By its light, Rosie could see that she had been pulled down behind a large boulder by a girl who looked very similar to the figure on the totem pole. The girl looked at Rosie and held a warning finger to her lips.

Rosie nodded and then cautiously peeped round the edge of the boulder to see what they were hiding from. At first, she couldn't see anything at all, but as she stared into the darkness she began to make out three shadowy shapes only metres away. Her skin prickled with goosebumps as she realized that they were hideous-looking monsters.

One of the monsters was enormous, with six or seven thick legs, and long feelers stretching out from its head. Another was smaller and more octopus-shaped. It squirmed along on a mass of tentacles and made a soft squelching sound as it moved. The third monster looked like an overgrown cockroach. It scuttled busily this way and that, its legs making horrible clicking noises and its antennae wiggling furiously.

Rosie kept completely still as she watched, her heart pounding. She hardly dared to breathe. The monsters all seemed to be looking for something – or someone. Were they hunting for the princess?

Rosie nervously withdrew behind the rock because the monsters were drawing closer and closer. Looking up, she could just see the largest monster's feelers appearing over the top of the boulder and hear it making low gulping sounds. Do the monsters want to eat us? Rosie wondered.

Then, abruptly, the monsters and the noises stopped. Rosie bit her lip nervously. Where had the monsters gone? Somehow the eerie silence was even worse than the gulping noises.

The princess gently nudged her and pointed at the sky. Rosie looked up and realized that the sun was starting to rise.

Streaks of orange light were spreading slowly into the dark blue of the night. As the sun rose higher and its rays glanced off the boulder, the little princess cautiously peeped over the top of the rock. Rosie did the same and saw that the monsters had completely vanished.

"They've gone," the princess said in a relieved voice. "Thank goodness!" she added as she stood up and stretched in the sunshine.

"What were they?" Rosie breathed.

"It's a long story," the princess sighed. Then she smiled. "I should probably introduce myself first. My name is Princess Malila."

Rosie smiled back and stood up. "And I'm Rosie. Hello. I came here by . . . well, by magic!"

Now that it was lighter, Rosie could get a proper look at the princess from the totem pole. She was dressed in a dark orange suede dress, edged with a beaded fringe. Around her waist was a belt, with a leather pouch attached to it. She had very long, dark hair neatly drawn into two plaits, and she wore a necklace of pretty silver and turquoise beads. Rosie looked down at herself and realized that she was wearing a tan suede skirt and top, also with fringing and beads. She touched her head and found that her unruly red curls were now in one long plait down her back.

The princess's pretty face had lit up upon hearing Rosie's name. "Did you really say Rosie?" she asked. "My grandmother used to tell me stories about being visited by a magical friend called Rosamund. Is that you?"

Rosie shook her head with a grin. "No. That must have been my great-aunt," she explained. "So what were those horrible monsters we were just hiding from?"

"Dream-shadows," Malila replied. Her dark eyes flashed angrily. "And they're just as horrible as they look! They come hunting for people at night to steal them away to the Shadow Lands." She shivered and rubbed her arms. "Now the sun is up, they have gone and we're safe – but only until nightfall comes again."

Rosie looked over the lush green plain that lay ahead of her. She and Malila were on a rocky path that ran alongside a wide, winding river. A black horse was tied to a tree nearby, and away in the distance were snow-topped mountains and dense pine forests.

"What were you doing out here in the night anyway?" Rosie asked curiously.

"I've come from the Arakami tribe," Malila told Rosie. She looked sad, but then she continued, and Rosie could hear determination in her voice. "Our camp is a day's ride from here. And I came because I'm trying to save my people."

Chapter Three

"Save them?" Rosie echoed. "Are they in danger?"

Malila nodded. "Come and meet Thunder and I'll tell you all about it," she said, striding over to the handsome black horse.

Rosie followed.
"Hello, boy," she said, patting Thunder's glossy flank. He bent his head and gave a low whinny in reply.

"The dream-shadows have been taking my people to the Shadow Lands, the place of bad dreams," Malila began. "Two days ago, they managed to take my father, the chief of our tribe."

"So are you going to the Shadow Lands to rescue everybody?" Rosie asked.

Malila shook her head. "No one knows where the Shadow Lands are," she replied. "No, I'm on the hunt for a thief." She untied Thunder's tether so that he could walk over to the river to drink. "You see, the dream-shadows didn't bother our tribe before because we had a dream-catcher in the village to protect us," she told Rosie. "But then it was stolen." She stopped as she saw Rosie's puzzled expression. "Do you know what a dream-catcher is?" she asked.

Rosie shook her head. "No," she admitted.

Malila held up her arms to form a circle

about the size of a dinner plate. "Our dream-catcher is about this big," she said. "It's a willow hoop with plant stems stretched across it, like a web. There are two feathers stitched into the centre – an owl feather for wisdom and an eagle feather for courage. The dream-catcher hangs in the centre of our camp and catches the dream-shadows from everybody's nightmares in its web."

"What happens to the dream-shadows?" Rosie asked, fascinated.

"When the first rays of the sun hit the dream-catcher each morning, the dream-shadows vanish," Malila replied. "But ever since our dream-catcher was stolen, we have had terrible nightmares and there is nothing to stop the dream-shadows roaming freely.

We light a fire in the centre of the village to keep them away because they are afraid of fire. But they're becoming more and more daring. Every night, they creep closer and our dreams get worse. And whenever they touch someone, that person vanishes with them into the Shadow Lands." Malila set her jaw determinedly. "That's why I'm tracking the thief. I need to get our dream-catcher back to stop the dream-shadows and to make sure our lost people are

returned to us."

"Can I help you?"

Rosie asked. "Maybe I could come with you?"

Malila smiled as she bent to fill her leather water-pouch from the river. "Oh, yes, I'd like that," she said eagerly. "It is lonely out here with just Thunder for company." She re-attached the water-pouch to the belt around her waist and grinned at Rosie. "Maybe you will bring me luck, and we will find the trickster coyote who took the dream-catcher. I've been tracking his paw-prints in the dust – see?"

She pointed down at the dusty track and Rosie nodded as she saw the paw-prints. "What kind of animal is a trickster coyote?"

she asked. She'd never
heard of such a creature
before.

Malila climbed onto Thunder's
back and reached a hand down
to help Rosie up behind her.
"Coyotes look a bit like dogs,"
she replied. "They are so cunning
and mischievous that they are
known as tricksters in our tribe."

Up on Thunder's back, Rosie
put her arms around Malila's waist.
Rosie remembered the large dog-like
creature on the totem pole and how playful
he looked. "How do you know it was a
coyote that took the dream-catcher?" she
asked Malila.

"There were coyote tracks leading away
from the tree where the dream-catcher used
to hang," the princess explained. Then she

made a clicking noise with her tongue, and
Thunder started to walk on along the
riverbank.

Rosie looked down at the paw-prints they
were following. "I hope we find him soon,"
she said, with feeling. "Because I *really* don't
want to meet any more of those dream-
shadows!"

"No," Malila agreed. "We need to find that
trickster!"

Chapter Four

It took Rosie a moment or two to get used to being on horseback without a saddle, but before long she was enjoying the ride. There were so many amazing things to see! First of all, Malila pointed out a family of beavers on the far side of the river, busily gnawing logs. Then she spotted a set of bear tracks that led off into the forest.

"A bear? Are we safe?" Rosie asked.

Malila nodded. "They are old tracks," she said confidently. "The bear passed this way three days ago, or more."

The sun was high in the sky now and it glinted off the water that tumbled over the rocky riverbed. A pair of bald eagles soared above them, their huge wings casting shadows on the path as they circled.

After a while, the coyote tracks turned away from the river and entered a forest. Here the pine trees provided shade from the hot sun. It was quieter, too, without the rushing of the river water.

The only sound, apart from the soft *thud, thud* of Thunder's hooves, was the occasional tapping of a

woodpecker against a tree.

"Where is that trickster going now?" Malila murmured, peering down to look at the ground more closely. Then, as they emerged into a sunny glade, she suddenly patted Thunder's flank. "Here!"

"What is it?" Rosie asked, as Thunder came to a stop.

Malila slipped down from her horse. "The tracks have stopped," she said in a low voice. "The coyote must be nearby."

Rosie scrambled off Thunder and looked around. Dappled sunlight streamed into the glade and birds called to one another from high up in the trees.

"Look," Malila whispered, pointing at

some white-flowered bushes. "The tracks lead into there."

Rosie bent down to peer into the bushes, noticing the sweet perfume of the white flowers as she did so. The leaves were a glossy dark green and each one had a distinctive sharp point at its tip. "Oh, yes," Rosie said in a whisper, spotting the trail of paw-prints threading through the bushes. "The coyote definitely went this way."

Malila quickly tethered Thunder to a tree, next to the flowering white bushes, and he instantly bent his head and munched on a couple of leaves. Then the two girls quietly made their way through the undergrowth, following the coyote's tracks.

Before long they had come to a small cave entrance. Malila raised her eyebrows and pointed inside. Rosie leaned forwards to see what her friend had spotted. Right at the back of the cave, the coyote was curled up, fast asleep on a bed of leaves. He looked very much like a large dog, Rosie thought, with his sandy brown coat and pointed ears.

Malila tiptoed into the coyote's den and Rosie followed. A little sunlight reached in through the leafy branches and dimly lit the interior of the cave. Rosie noticed that the glossy leaves from the bushes outside lined the floor of the coyote's home. But there was no sign of the Arakami's dream-catcher anywhere!

Rosie crept further into the cave, wondering if it might be in one of the dark corners right at the back. But she hadn't gone far when she heard a loud *snap!* Rosie turned and saw Malila, frozen in alarm, a broken twig beneath one foot.

Both girls turned anxiously to the coyote, willing him not to stir. But it was too late.

His pointed ears had pricked up and he
opened his eyes. When he saw
Rosie and Malila standing in
his cave, he jumped to his
feet and growled
menacingly at
them.

Chapter Five

Rosie's fear quickly turned to astonishment. She could understand the coyote's growls just as clearly as if he were speaking to her!

"Who are you? What are you doing in my cave?" he was growling.

Rosie glanced at Malila, wondering if she was imagining all this, but Malila's eyes were wide with shock, too. Clearly they could both understand the coyote.

"At least introduce yourselves," the coyote said, sounding exasperated. "Don't you humans have any manners?" He switched his long tail from side to side crossly, sending leaves flying. "It's very rude for guests to turn up unannounced and sneak around while someone's sleeping! What do you want?"

Malila coughed, and cleared her throat. "Um . . . hello," she said hesitantly, clearly surprised to find herself in conversation with a coyote.

"Hello?" the coyote scoffed. "*Hello?* It's a bit late for that, isn't it? I was brought up to say hello *before* I walked into someone's home, not afterwards." He looked from Malila to Rosie and rolled his eyes. "Honestly!"

Despite the coyote's bluster, Rosie could see that he was shuffling his paws nervously, almost as if he were hiding something. She wondered if he had guessed that they had come looking for the dream-catcher.

"Hello, I'm Rosie," she said politely. "And

this is Malila. We're very sorry that we walked into your cave without asking."

The coyote wagged his tail merrily at her. "That's all right — you just gave me a bit of a fright, that's all. And you can call me Coyote," he said, sounding much friendlier.

"But, Coyote, how is it that you can understand what we're saying?" Rosie asked.

"And how is it that *we* can understand what *you're* saying?" Malila added.

Coyote sighed as if the girls were quite brainless. "Because of *these*, of course," he said, pushing a few of

the glossy green leaves towards the girls with his paw.

Rosie bent down to pick one up, wondering what the leaves could do. But Malila was nodding in recognition.

"The shaman of our tribe often talks about these leaves," she exclaimed in delight, turning one of them over in her hand. "They are known as Hear-Me leaves because they give humans and animals the power to communicate with each other." She shook her head as if she could hardly believe she was holding one. "They are very rare, and I have never seen one before. I thought it was just a legend, but the shaman was right!"

Rosie couldn't help smiling. "Well, it's lucky we can all understand each other, Coyote," she said sweetly. "Because now you can tell us where the Arakami dream-catcher is!"

Coyote looked at the ground. "The dream-what?" he asked, rather unconvincingly.

Malila put her hands on her hips and her dark eyes flashed. She clearly wasn't fooled for an instant. "The dream-catcher," she said. "I have followed your tracks from my camp, Coyote. I know you took it, and my tribe needs it back before it's too late."

Coyote squirmed under Malila's fierce gaze, until eventually he looked away sheepishly. "What do you mean, 'too late'?" he asked.

Malila quickly explained what had been happening to her people since the coming of the dream shadows, and Coyote looked even more uncomfortable.

Then he sighed. "All right," he said, hanging his head. "I did take the dream-catcher. You see, I'm only a young coyote and I'm still learning how to become a wily trickster. I took the dream-catcher to impress the Great Trickster Spirit." He looked at the girls beseechingly. "But I didn't realize that those monsters would come and take away your people! I'd never have done it if I'd known!"

Rosie gave Coyote a comforting pat. He did look very sorry.

"I'm not cross," Malila told him. "I just want the dream-catcher back, that's all. If you give it back, everything will be all right again."

Coyote's ears drooped. "I was hoping you weren't going to say that," he confessed.

"Why?" Rosie asked.

"Because I haven't got the dream-catcher any more," Coyote explained. "I've already given it away — to the Great Trickster Spirit!"

Chapter Six

Malila stared at him. "Given it away?" she echoed in horror.

There was silence as Coyote nodded, looking downcast.

"So where is this Great Trickster Spirit?" Rosie asked. "And what does he look like? We'll have to go and ask him to give the dream-catcher back."

"The Great Trickster Spirit normally appears as a big coyote, but he's really much more than that. He is a very powerful spirit and he lives in the magic Spirit Lands,

behind the Great Waterfall," Coyote replied.
"I can take you there," he offered, looking
brighter. "You'll never find your way without
a guide."

Rosie looked over at Malila, who was
nodding.

"We have to try," the little princess said
firmly. "And we'd better take some of these
leaves with us so that we can carry on
understanding each other." She stooped and
picked up a handful of the glossy green
leaves and deftly wove them into
headbands. She put one on her
own head, one on
Rosie's and one
on Coyote's.

Coyote gave a happy bark. "Does it suit me?" he asked cheekily, putting his head on one side.

Rosie and Malila couldn't help laughing.

"Green is definitely your colour," Rosie assured him as they headed out of the cave.

Rosie, Malila and Coyote made their way back to Thunder, who looked up from the leaves he was eating as they approached. "You found the trickster, I see," Thunder neighed in a deep voice, and Rosie jumped in surprise.

Malila looked astonished, too — and then both girls found themselves smiling. "Thunder, you clever horse, you ate the Hear-Me leaves and now we can talk to each other!" Malila cried, throwing her arms around his neck. "Can you take us a bit further, please?" she asked him.

"Coyote's going to show us the way."

"Of course," Thunder replied, bowing his great head.

Rosie and Malila climbed onto Thunder's back and set off after Coyote, who was bounding along the path.

Coyote led them deeper and deeper into the forest. "I hope this isn't another trick," Rosie whispered to Malila. "We've been riding for ages now."

Before Malila could reply, both girls heard a faint splashing sound ahead of them.

"Sounds like a waterfall to me," Thunder said, his black ears twitching.

Coyote looked back over his shoulder. "Nearly there," he yapped cheerfully.

The sound grew louder until they emerged from the trees to see a spectacular waterfall right in front of them.

"Wow!" breathed Rosie, spellbound by the

sight. Shining sheets of water plunged down the rock face and spray glittered in the sunlight, sending rainbows dancing around the edges of the cascade. The torrent splashed down into a deep blue pool.

Rosie slid off Thunder's back and scooped up some of the water from the pool to drink. It was icy cold, clear and delicious.

Malila dismounted, too, and led Thunder to the pool. He drank gratefully while Malila used the water to wipe down his hot neck.

"You'll have to finish the journey on foot," Coyote told them. "We need to climb up and go behind the waterfall to enter the Spirit Lands."

"Be careful on those slippery rocks," Thunder neighed, his brown eyes concerned, as he looked at Malila.

"We will," Malila said, hugging him. "And

we'll come back for you as soon as we can."

"Come on, then," Coyote said, bounding eagerly up the first few rocks. "Let's go!"

Rosie and Malila picked their way from rock to rock as they followed Coyote up the steep rock face. Thunder had been right, the rocks were slippery, and Rosie held on tightly as she climbed.

Eventually, they reached a stone ledge which ran behind the falling water. Coyote leaped onto it, and both girls scrambled after him.

Rosie glanced down to see how far they'd come, and her head spun as she saw how tiny Thunder looked down on the ground below. She realized that they were very high up now, so high she was actually looking down on the treetops.

The girls followed Coyote behind the waterfall and along a dark rocky passage.

The noise of the water receded as the passage wound its way deeper into the mountainside, and then there was silence.

"Here we are," Coyote said, as the path emerged into daylight again.

The girls followed him, and Rosie caught her breath as she gazed at the beautiful valley before her. Lush, grassy meadows bordered a babbling stream, and exotic-looking birds darted among the wild flowers, their feathers flashing sapphire and emerald in the sunshine.

"Oh, how beautiful!" Rosie said, blinking in the bright light.

"This way," Coyote called, already trotting ahead.

Rosie and Malila followed him over to a little spinney of trees, hung with all kinds of sparkling treasures: jewels, mirrors, beads and bells.

"Everything here is so pretty!" Rosie laughed, tipping her head back to gaze at the glittering

trinkets that dangled above her head.

Then something caught Rosie's attention. She shaded her eyes from the sun and peered up at the highest branch of the tallest tree. There, turning in the breeze, she could see something that looked very much like Malila's description of a dream-catcher. "Malila, look!" she cried, pointing upwards.

Malila gazed up into the tree, and then her face broke into a grin. "The dream-catcher!" she cried in delight. "We've found it!"

Chapter Seven

Malila ran to the bottom of the tree and immediately began to climb. "Luckily I'm the best tree-climber in the whole of the Arakami tribe," she said happily as she made her way upwards.

Coyote and Rosie watched anxiously as Malila climbed higher.

"Be careful," Coyote called. "With the Great Trickster, things are never quite what they seem!"

But Malila kept climbing. "That definitely looks like the Arakami dream-catcher," she said firmly. "And nothing is going to stop me taking it back to our camp!"

As Malila climbed higher, Rosie noticed that the birdsong around them had died away. It was as if all the birds in the valley were watching the brave princess climbing the tree.

"She won't do it, you know," Coyote said in a low voice to Rosie.

"What do you mean? Of course she will!" Rosie

replied indignantly. "Look at her – she's a brilliant climber!"

Coyote shook his head. "Even if she was the best climber in the world, she wouldn't be able to reach that dream-catcher," he said sadly.

Rosie gazed upwards with a frown. Malila was certainly very high up in the tree now, but she didn't actually seem to be any nearer to the dream-catcher. Somehow, it was still a long way out of reach.

But a tree can't grow taller just like that, can it? Rosie thought. Surely if Malila goes on climbing she'll reach the dream-catcher eventually?

As Rosie looked up at her friend, her eyes were drawn to one of the dangling treasures on a branch above her head. It was a pretty pink glass bauble, spangled with sparkling silver stars. Impulsively, Rosie stood on tiptoe

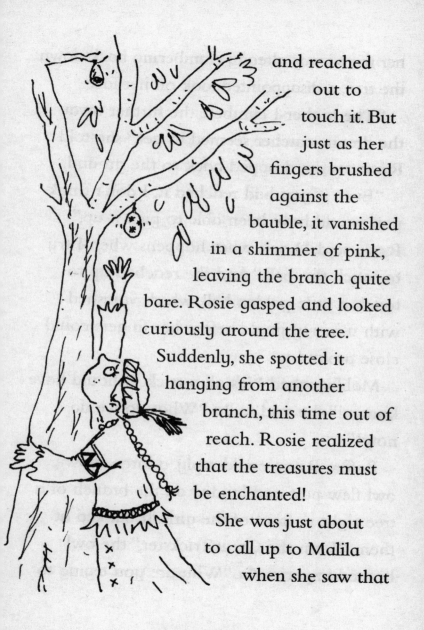

and reached out to touch it. But just as her fingers brushed against the bauble, it vanished in a shimmer of pink, leaving the branch quite bare. Rosie gasped and looked curiously around the tree. Suddenly, she spotted it hanging from another branch, this time out of reach. Rosie realized that the treasures must be enchanted! She was just about to call up to Malila when she saw that her friend was already clambering back down the tree, a disappointed look on her face.

"The higher I climbed, the further away the dream-catcher seemed to get," she told Rosie, as she dropped back to the ground.

"Even if you had reached it, I don't think you would have been able to pick it up," Rosie said. "Look what happens when I try to touch this bell." And she reached up to touch a little golden bell, which vanished with a merry jingle before her fingers could close around it.

Malila sighed. "It's all a trick. I should have known!" she said sadly. "What do we do now?"

Before Rosie could reply, a large snowy owl flew past and landed on the branch of a tree right in front of the girls. It blinked at them. "I am the Great Trickster," the owl hooted imperiously. "Why are you trying to

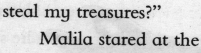

steal my treasures?"

Malila stared at the owl in confusion. "I thought the Great Trickster was supposed to be a coyote," she said. She had hardly finished her sentence when the owl flew to the ground and changed into a magnificent coyote! The Great Trickster Spirit sat down facing the girls. "Why have you come to the Spirit Lands?" he asked in a deep voice. "What is it that you seek?"

Rosie felt a little nervous. The Great Trickster coyote was huge compared to their friendly little coyote, and she could see his sharp white teeth when he spoke.

If Malila was nervous, she didn't show it.

"I've come for the Arakami dream-catcher," she said in a clear voice. "I need it for my people, before the dream-shadows take everyone to the Shadow Lands."

The Great Trickster looked thoughtful for a moment. Then he stood up on all fours and stretched. As he did so, his body changed again – this time the girls found themselves looking at a huge grizzly bear!

Rosie, Malila and Coyote all stepped back in alarm.

"If you want your dream-catcher back," the bear rumbled, "you will need to give me something better in return."

Rosie's heart was beating fast, but she stepped forward bravely. "What would you like, Great Trickster?" she asked.

The bear shook himself, then stood up on his hind legs. "Bring me the tail of a shooting star!" he commanded. "But bring it to me by sunrise." A smile spread across his furry face. "Otherwise I will keep the dream-catcher for ever."

The girls gazed at the bear in horror. "But how—?" Malila began, but she was interrupted by the Great Trickster.

"Good luck," he rumbled. And without another word, his bear body dissolved right before their eyes, turning into hundreds of rainbow-coloured butterflies that fluttered away on the breeze.

Rosie, Malila and Coyote could only stare as the butterflies scattered across the valley. Then they turned to look at each other in dismay. How were they ever going to catch the tail of a shooting star?

Chapter Eight

Malila looked helplessly at Rosie and Coyote ."How are we supposed to reach the stars?" she asked. "Surely it's impossible!"

Coyote suddenly wagged his tail and began bounding around the girls excitedly. "I have a great idea," he announced. "My friend, Eagle, is certain to help us. Follow me!"

Rosie and Malila looked at each other hopefully and then rushed after Coyote. He led them to a clearing not far away, where an enormous bald eagle sat on an old tree stump, grooming his feathers with his sharp, curved beak. The eagle was so huge that Rosie and Malila had to crane their necks back to look at him properly.

"Eagles aren't usually that big, are they?" Rosie asked Malila in a surprised whisper as they approached the huge bird.

Malila shook her head. "This must be some kind of magical eagle," she hissed in reply.

Coyote barked a greeting and the eagle turned to look at him.

Rosie was standing next to Coyote and he nudged her hand. "Give Eagle some of the Hear-Me leaves," he said. "Then he'll be able to understand you and Malila."

Rosie obediently took a couple of leaves from her headband and held them out to the eagle. She couldn't help feeling a little nervous — the eagle's beak looked very sharp, after all — but Eagle plucked the leaves gently

from Rosie's hand and swallowed them in a single gulp. Then he folded his wings behind him.

"Hello," he said, in a scratchy sort of voice. "What brings you here today?" Then he looked at the girls closely. "Coyote isn't tricking you, is he?" he asked them. "You don't want to trust this one if you can help it!"

Rosie smothered a chuckle as Coyote looked embarrassed.

"Well, to be honest, I did get them into a bit of trouble," Coyote confessed, "so I was rather hoping that you'd help me get them out of it again . . ."

Eagle gave a short, dry cough of a laugh – as if he wasn't at all surprised by Coyote's confession. Rosie had the feeling this wasn't the first time Coyote had come to the great bird seeking a favour.

Malila stepped forward. "We really need your help, great eagle," she explained. "We have to catch the tail of a shooting star for the Great Trickster, before sunrise."

Eagle drew himself up, looking thoughtful. Then he grinned. "A shooting star, eh?" he mused. "I'll have to fly very fast for that – which is just what I like doing best!"

"So you'll help us?" Rosie asked hopefully.

Eagle turned his kindly eyes upon Rosie and nodded. "Of course I'll help." He gestured to the sky with his head. "Dusk is falling already," he said. "The stars will be out very soon. Why don't you climb up on my back and we'll try to catch an early one."

The girls nodded happily and the eagle hopped down to the ground and spread out his enormous wings. He looked at Coyote. "Will you be coming, my young friend?"

Coyote shook his head. "I don't think coyotes are meant to fly," he replied. "I'll just wait here."

Coyote curled up to wait for the girls while they climbed carefully up onto Eagle's back.

The great bird turned his head and gave them a reassuring wink. "Ready for takeoff?" he asked.

"Yes, please," Rosie said, holding on to the eagle's powerful shoulders and waving at Coyote.

"Goodbye, Coyote!" Malila called.

"Good luck!" Coyote replied, as the eagle flapped his mighty wings once . . . twice . . . and then took off, shooting steeply upwards.

Wind rushed past Rosie's face as the eagle soared across the twilight sky, his powerful wings beating rhythmically. The sky was darkening fast, turning to indigo blue. And

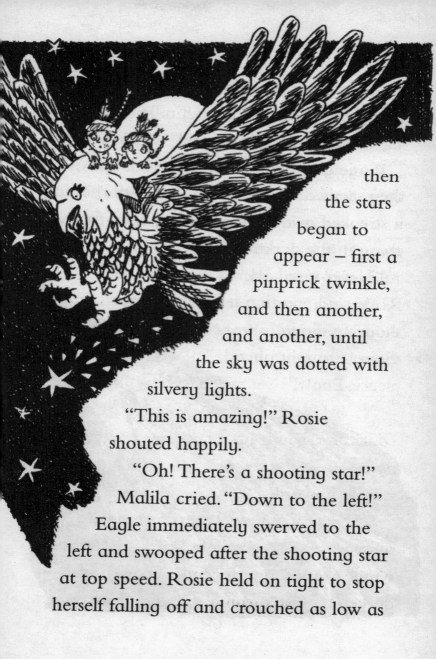

then
the stars
began to
appear – first a
pinprick twinkle,
and then another,
and another, until
the sky was dotted with
silvery lights.

"This is amazing!" Rosie
shouted happily.

"Oh! There's a shooting star!"
Malila cried. "Down to the left!"
Eagle immediately swerved to the
left and swooped after the shooting star
at top speed. Rosie held on tight to stop
herself falling off and crouched as low as

she could over his shoulders. It was like being on the fastest, most exciting rollercoaster ever.

"Get ready to grab its tail!" Malila shouted.

Rosie got ready to lean out, but just as they seemed to be catching up with the star, it streaked away across the sky, then fizzled away in the darkness.

"Never mind, there's another one!" Rosie said, spotting a dazzling light shooting along in front of them. "Straight ahead, please, Eagle!"

Once again, Eagle
zoomed towards
the shooting
                                    star so fast
                              that Rosie
                        thought they must catch
                    up with it. But, once again,
                the star was swifter still, leaving
            only a glimmering silver trail, which
was impossible to catch.

"I see another," Eagle called back to the
girls, as the second star faded into the
blackness. He whizzed after the third
shooting star, and Rosie found herself
laughing in excitement as once more the
wind rushed past her ears.

This star didn't seem in any rush to burn
out. In fact, it led Eagle a merry dance all
over the sky, twisting and turning,
tantalizingly just ahead of them – always too

far away to reach. A faint chuckle floated through the air and Rosie stared at the star in surprise. Was she hearing things, or was the star actually chuckling with glee as it darted to and fro?

Impulsively, she called out, "Star, don't run away! Please can we catch your tail?"

"Rosie!" Malila laughed. "Why are you talking to a star? Stars can't speak."

Rosie strained her ears into the darkness, listening for the laughter again or, better still, a reply, but she only heard the whistle of the wind past her ears. "I was sure that I heard the star laughing," she told Malila, suddenly feeling a bit silly, "but it must have been the wind."

At that moment, the girls heard a silvery voice echo across the sky. "Why do you want to catch me?" it said. The star was actually talking to them!

Malila clutched Rosie's arm in surprise. "Did you hear that?" she cried.

"Yes!" Rosie gasped.

"Star, the Great Trickster has set us a challenge," Malila called out quickly. "He's asked us to fetch him the tail of a shooting star."

A tinkling laugh floated down to the girls. "The tail of a shooting star cannot be caught," the star replied. "Not by anyone. Stars are too wise to be caught by humans.

And a powerful spirit like the Great Trickster knows that."

Rosie felt her shoulders slump as she listened, and she heard Malila sigh disappointedly behind her. So they had been tricked by the Great Trickster again!

But the star hadn't finished. "A shooting star only appears when a star is about to say goodbye," it went on. "We stars give one last fiery display before we sleep for ever. So, even if a shooting star were to be caught, its light would wink out well before it reached the ground." The star chuckled again. "You've been tricked, my dears," it told the girls. "You'll have to think of a way to turn the Great Trickster's trick around!"

"Thank you, Star," Rosie called out. "The star's right," she shouted back to Malila. "We will need to trick the Great Trickster into giving us back the dream-catcher — but how?"

Malila leaned forwards. "Eagle, please will you take us down to the ground again?" she asked the great bird. "We've got to think up a plan – and fast!"

Rosie racked her brains as the mighty eagle swooped downwards. There had to be some way to beat the Great Trickster. If *only* she could think of it . . .

Coyote was waiting for them expectantly, but his ears drooped when he saw the girls clamber down empty-handed. "No luck?" he asked, sounding despondent.

Malila shook her head. "It was all a trick," she told him.

The girls thanked Eagle for his help.

"My pleasure," he replied. "I am sorry that we didn't catch the tail of a shooting star, but we had fun, didn't we?" The girls nodded and waved goodbye as Eagle took off again and soared away on the breeze.

Both girls gazed after him, lost in thought. Then Malila gave a little gasp. "The sky is lightening," she cried, pointing upwards. "We must get back to the Great Trickster before the sun rises."

"But we don't have the tail of a star to give him," Coyote protested. "And he won't give the dream-catcher back without it."

Suddenly, Coyote's words gave Rosie an idea. "The tail of a star . . ." she murmured thoughtfully. "That's it!" she cried, grinning at her friends and breaking into a run. "Come on!"

Chapter Nine

"What is it?" Malila shouted, racing to catch up with Rosie. "What are you going to do?"

"Let's just get there first," Rosie replied breathlessly. "We don't have much time!"

As the three of them reached the Great Trickster's spinney of trees, Rosie saw the dream-catcher spinning on its high branch against the pink of the morning sky. And then, as the sun edged up over the horizon, she spotted the Great Trickster loping towards them in his coyote form.

Rosie took a deep breath. "Please sit

down," she told the Great Trickster, in as
confident a voice as she could muster. "For
we have brought you the tale of a shooting
star!"

Malila
turned
anxiously
towards
her
friend.
"But
Rosie—" she began.

"Don't worry, we just have to play the
Great Trickster at his own game," Rosie
hissed, as the Great Trickster sat down with a
curious look on his face.

"If you're comfortable, then I'll begin my
tale," Rosie declared grandly. "Once upon a
time, there was a great eagle who lived in the
Spirit Lands. One day, two girls came to him

and asked him to fly them up to the sky, for they needed to catch a shooting star." She paused for breath, hoping her plan was going to work. "The eagle flew the girls up as high as he could go and they zoomed around the heavens together, chasing shooting stars – but they couldn't catch a single one! One of the girls called out to a shooting star and begged it to let her catch its tail, but the star only laughed and told the girls that it was impossible. 'Nobody can catch a shooting star,' it told them."

Rosie quickly looked over at Malila and Coyote, who both smiled at her encouragingly. But her heart sank when she looked at the Great Trickster. His face was stony and he didn't look at all impressed with her tale so far. Rosie carried on bravely. "The star explained to the girls that all stars live long, happy lives, shining and sparkling in the

night sky. Just
before they fall asleep
for ever, they rush to the
ground in a final blaze of
fiery sparks. This final goodbye
is what you see when you
glimpse a shooting star. The girls
now understood that the sparkle of a
shooting star's tail would fade and die
almost immediately, even if they *could* catch
it! So they thanked the wise star for its words
and the eagle flew them back down to the
ground as the star faded away in a shower of
golden sparks. The End."

Rosie smiled nervously at the Great
Trickster. "There," she said. "I've given you
the tale of a shooting star, so now you must
return the dream-catcher to Malila!"

The Great Trickster was silent for a
moment. Rosie held her breath, wondering

how he was going to respond to her trick.
What if he was angry?

The Great Trickster tipped his head to one
side, his eyes still upon Rosie. He twitched his
tail, and said, "Tail!" Then he looked at
Rosie, and said, "Tale!" And then the Great
Trickster was laughing. "Very good," he
chuckled delightedly. His tail was
wagging now. "Very good! I
asked for a tail — and you
gave me a
tale!"

Malila
stepped forward. "Does this mean . . .?"
she began hopefully.

The Great Trickster smiled and nodded
his head towards the nearest tree. It
shimmered with a golden light and then
Rosie saw that there, on its lowest branch,

hung Malila's dream-catcher.

"Thank you!" Malila cried, running over at once. She lifted it down and ran her fingers over it lovingly. Then she smiled in relief. "Now my village will be safe again," she said, as she looped the dream-catcher around her neck.

The Great Trickster nodded, then turned and loped away. Rosie could hear him still chuckling to himself as he went. "Tail, tale – that's a good one!"

Coyote bounced up to Rosie, his own tail wagging in a fluffy blur. "That was a brilliant idea, Rosie!" he cried happily.

Malila flung her arms around Rosie. "You're a genius," she said, hugging her. "Your plan worked!"

"We've got the dream-catcher," Rosie replied, hugging Malila back. "So let's take it back to where it belongs right away!"

Malila nodded and the three of them headed joyfully back to the waterfall, where Thunder was waiting. He whickered happily when he saw the dream-catcher, and Malila and Rosie told him all about their adventure as they climbed onto his back and headed for home. Coyote trotted alongside, putting in any details that the girls had forgotten.

The journey back to the Arakami camp was much quicker than Malila's journey out had been, because the princess didn't need to look for tracks any more. But it was still a long day's ride. The friends had not quite reached the camp when the sun began to sink in the sky.

"It's not much further now," Malila said. "Look, I can see the tops of the tepees – and

there's the earth-lodge."

"What's an earth-lodge?" Rosie asked, peering over Malila's shoulder to see.

"It's where most of us live," Malila replied. "It's a long cabin, built with logs and clay, and there are different rooms for different families." She glanced up at the sky, then urged Thunder on. "It's getting dark quickly," she said nervously as the sun sank lower behind the mountains and the light began to

fade. "If we don't get back to the village soon and put the dream-catcher back in its place, the dream-shadows will come out."

As the princess spoke, Rosie saw a movement out of the corner of her eye and turned to see a large, many-legged creature slinking around in the shadows. "I think it's too late — look over there," Rosie said to Malila, pointing into the gloom. "And I think it's just seen us," she added nervously, as the monster turned and moved in their direction.

"Hurry, Thunder!" Malila cried, and her horse obediently galloped faster towards the Arakami camp.

"It's following us," Rosie cried, as the

dream-shadow began to chase after them. Rosie could hear its claws clicking on the ground as it ran. Coyote was barking at it angrily, but the monster took no notice. It seemed only interested in Rosie and Malila.

"Keep going, Thunder," Malila urged. "We're nearly there!" They were so close to the village now that Rosie could smell food cooking on the campfires. But around the edge of the camp, she could see ominous shapes lurking in the shadows.

"Look out, more dream-shadows!" she warned Malila.

Thunder stumbled on a rock. He was tiring, Rosie realized, and no wonder: he had travelled a long way. "Can we use the dream-catcher to chase away the dream-shadows?" she called out to the princess.

But Malila shook her head grimly. "It only works when it's in its proper place in the centre of the camp," she replied. "It's powerless until we can get it there." She

took the dream-catcher from around her neck and passed it to Rosie. "If I guide Thunder to the dream-catcher tree, will you hang it up for me?"

"Of course," Rosie agreed, clutching it with one hand as she clung to Malila with the other.

There were two dream-shadows chasing them now. And another one at the edge of the camp seemed to have spotted them, too. With a last burst of energy, Thunder ran on, swerving to avoid the monsters as he charged right into the centre of the Arakami camp.

"We're coming up to the tree," Malila shouted over her shoulder as they galloped past what had to be the earth-lodge. "This way, Thunder, you can do it!"

Rosie could see the tree that Malila

meant. It was a single pine tree, surrounded by tepees on three sides, and the earth-lodge on the fourth. They were nearly there. We're going to make it! she thought excitedly.

But just then, she felt hot breath on her right leg. And as Thunder hurtled towards the pine tree, Rosie looked down to see a dream-shadow level with her, and reaching out for her leg with shadowy claws.

She shrieked and drew her leg up away from it, almost tumbling off Thunder's back in the process. Coyote growled menacingly at the monster, but it merely howled in reply and stretched even further towards Rosie.

Chapter Ten

Rosie leaned away as far as she could without falling off Thunder, and held the dream-catcher at the ready.

Malila guided her horse up to the tree. "Now, Rosie!" she called.

Her heart thumping, Rosie saw that there was one branch that stuck straight out from the trunk. She looped the dream-catcher over it with trembling fingers, all the while expecting to feel the dream-shadow grab hold of her.

But as soon as it was back in its place, the

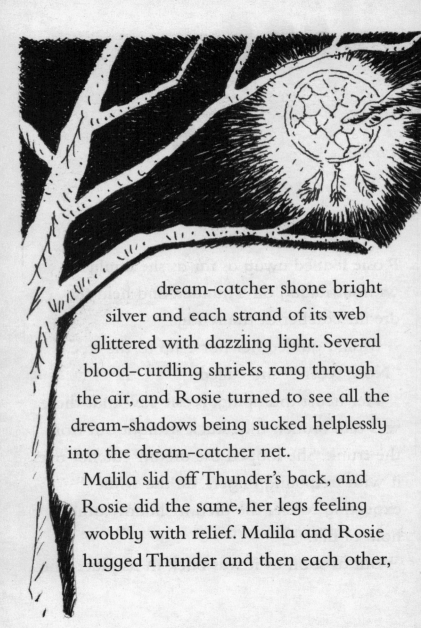

dream-catcher shone bright
silver and each strand of its web
glittered with dazzling light. Several
blood-curdling shrieks rang through
the air, and Rosie turned to see all the
dream-shadows being sucked helplessly
into the dream-catcher net.

Malila slid off Thunder's back, and
Rosie did the same, her legs feeling
wobbly with relief. Malila and Rosie
hugged Thunder and then each other,

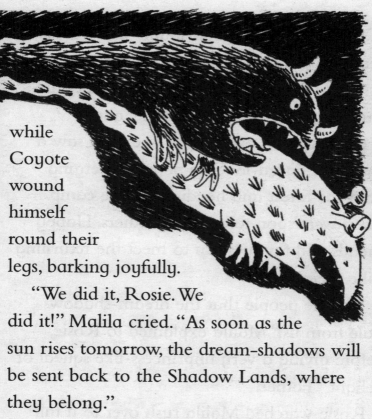

while
Coyote
wound
himself
round their
legs, barking joyfully.

"We did it, Rosie. We did it!" Malila cried. "As soon as the sun rises tomorrow, the dream-shadows will be sent back to the Shadow Lands, where they belong."

Rosie heard cheers and looked up to see several people running towards them. Others were emerging from tepees and the earth-lodge, surprised and delighted to see the dream-catcher safely back in its place.

The happy cries grew louder and people began to point to the forest excitedly.

Malila turned to look. "The lost ones are returning!" she exclaimed in delight.

Rosie looked over to the trees and saw a couple of dazed-looking people emerging from the forest and heading for the camp. They were soon followed by others. Happy friends and families ran to meet the returning tribe members.

"It's the people that the dream-shadows stole from us," Malila explained to Rosie, before giving a very unprincess-like squeal of delight. "Father!"

Rosie watched Malila rush over to a tall man, who scooped her up in his arms and swung her round.

"I love a happy ending," Coyote said cheerfully.

Rosie reached down to stroke his fur. "So

do I," she said, grinning as Malila and her father walked over to them.

"Father, this is Rosie and Coyote," Malila said, her eyes shining with happiness. "And this is my father, Hakan, Chief of the Arakami tribe." She was still holding his hand. "It's thanks to Rosie and Coyote that we have the dream-catcher back in the village," she added.

Coyote nuzzled Malila's free hand, and Rosie guessed that he was grateful Malila hadn't mentioned who it was that took the dream-catcher in the first place!

The Arakami Chief smiled warmly at Rosie and Coyote. "We owe you much," he said. "I am pleased to be back with my people – and we are all grateful that the dream-catcher has been returned. Thank you." He leaned down to pat Coyote, who wagged his tail.

Rosie smiled at Malila. "I think I should go," she said reluctantly, as Malila's father went to greet his people. She crouched down to hug Coyote goodbye. "I've had such fun with you both," she said, and Coyote nuzzled affectionately at her cheek.

"Thank you, Rosie," Malila said, hugging her friend. "You will always be an honoured guest of the Arakami people. Please come back and visit us soon."

"I will," Rosie promised. "Goodbye!" As soon as the word left her lips, she was swept up in the pine-scented whirlwind again, and she closed her eyes.

When the whirlwind stopped, Rosie opened her eyes to see that she was back in the maze, in front of the totem pole. Curiously, she examined the pictures on the pole. The princess was smiling now, and the coyote was running beside her horse, his tail in the air.

Rosie blinked. For a split-second, it had seemed as if the princess had waved to her. She rubbed her eyes and looked again. The princess was quite still now. "I'll see you again soon!" Rosie whispered to Malila and Coyote.

Suddenly, she heard her brother's voice through the hedge. "And Luke Campbell is almost out of the maze . . ." he was shouting breathlessly, as if he were a commentator watching the race.

The race! thought Rosie with a start. Of course! She glanced back at the totem pole for a second, and then decided to run in the direction that the princess and coyote were facing. There was still a chance that she might be able to catch up with Luke.

Luckily, the princess had been facing the right way. Minutes later, Rosie spotted the exit ahead of her, just as Luke came hurtling towards it from the other direction.

"And Luke Campbell takes the gold!" he shouted, beaming all over his face as he just beat Rosie out of the maze. He threw himself onto the grass, panting. "And you know what that means, don't you?" he added cheekily, sitting up once he'd caught his breath. "You have to tidy my bedroom for me!" Rosie laughed. She didn't mind too much. "Come on, then," she said, "let's go and find those dinosaurs."

Luke cheered and set off towards the castle, with Rosie in pursuit. And I'll definitely keep my eyes open while I'm tidying, she thought to herself with a smile. Because who knows where I'll find my next little princess?

THE END

Did you enjoy reading about Rosie's
adventure with the Dream-catcher Princess?
If you did, you'll love the
next *Little Princesses* book!

Turn over to read the first chapter of
The Desert Princess.

Chapter 1

"Is it time to go yet, Dad?" Rosie asked, hurrying into the castle kitchen, where her father and her younger brother, Luke, were sitting at the enormous pine table. "I don't want to be late."

Her father laughed. "You asked me that five minutes ago!" he pointed out. "If we leave now, we'll be too early!"

"Sorry," Rosie said, and grinned. "I'm just so excited about Emma's party. Everyone at school's been talking about it."

"You look different," Luke said, staring at Rosie's costume. She wore a long golden dress, a thin gold headband and armfuls of bangles.

"Mum made the dress from some bits of material we found in Great-aunt Rosamund's sewing room," Rosie explained.

Luke nodded wisely. "I know what you're dressed as," he said proudly. "An ancient eruption!"

Rosie and Mr Campbell burst out laughing.

"Nearly right!" Rosie said. "An ancient *Egyptian*!"

"Can I see the invitation again?" Luke asked eagerly. "It had funny pictures on it!"

Rosie pulled a glossy cream card from the pocket of her dress and laid it on the table. All the details for the party were listed in bright gold lettering, and then underneath it said, "Could all guests come as glittering ancient Egyptian princes and princesses?" Around the edges of the invitation there were lots of ancient Egyptian drawings, including one of a pharaoh dressed in white and gold robes, with an elaborate headdress.

"What's that, Dad?" Rosie asked, pointing at a picture of a fabulous cat-like beast. It had the body of a lion, a human head and large wings folded neatly against its sides.

"That's the Sphinx!" replied Mr Campbell. "He's a legendary beast, and there's an enormous stone statue of him in Egypt, next to the Pyramids. According to the myths, the Sphinx would stop travellers who were passing and ask them to solve a riddle. If they failed, he would swallow them whole!"

"Oh!" Rosie clapped a hand to her mouth. "I knew there was something I'd forgotten! Mum said I could borrow some of her glittery eye-shadow."

"Don't trip over your dress!" called Mr Campbell, as Rosie dashed out of the kitchen. "We've got plenty of time."

Rosie picked up her skirt and hurried up the main staircase next to the Great Hall. Her parents' bedroom was the biggest of all the rooms on the second floor. It had a four-poster bed, draped with pale-lilac curtains patterned with glittering blue and green peacocks.

Rosie found the pot of eye-shadow on the dressing table and began to apply it carefully. When she'd finished, she stared at herself in the mirror. Now I really do look like an ancient Egyptian! she thought. Her gaze suddenly fell on a small picture hanging beside the mirror. It was an ancient Egyptian painting on papyrus.

"I can't believe I've never noticed that before!" Rosie said to herself, taking a closer look.

The picture showed a young girl, wearing a white silk dress decorated with gold thread.

The girl's face was sad, even though two cats, one black and one ginger, sat at her feet, their tails curled neatly round their bodies. Rosie looked at the cats closely and noticed that they looked rather unhappy, too.

"It's another little princess!" Rosie gasped, staring at the gold jewellery the girl was wearing. "It *must* be!"

Her heart thumping with excitement, Rosie bobbed a curtsey. "Hello," she said, just as her Great-aunt Rosamund had instructed in the note.

At once a warm breeze streamed out of the painting and swirled around Rosie. The breeze was heavy with the smell of exotic perfume, and it sparkled with tiny grains of golden sand. Rosie closed her eyes as the breeze grew stronger and lifted her up off the floor.

A few seconds later, Rosie's feet touched the ground again, and the breeze that had brought her died away. Rosie could feel the heat of the sun on her face and hear the gentle lapping of water even before she opened her eyes. When she did open them, she found herself blinking in bright sunshine as she looked around eagerly.

"Oh!" Rosie gasped.

She was standing on the bank of a mighty river, and slender reeds swayed gently in the light breeze. In the distance she could see a dazzling white building surrounded by lush green gardens. Beyond that, a village of small houses nestled in the shade of palm trees, before the landscape changed into the bronze sands of the desert, which stretched away in every direction.

"Where am I?" Rosie said to herself. Her

dress billowed around her in a gust of wind and she realized that her clothes had changed. She now wore a long, pale-blue robe and gold bands on her arms and ankles. Curiously, Rosie put a hand to her head and found that her hair was braided into lots of thin plaits, sealed with brightly coloured beads.

Just then, Rosie noticed a girl kneeling on the riverbank not far away. Two cats, one black, one ginger, sat quietly beside her, their long tails waving.

Rosie's heart missed a beat. I must be in ancient Egypt because that's the little princess from the painting! she thought excitedly. She looks sad. Maybe I can help her!

Determined to find out what was wrong, Rosie hurried over to the girl. As she drew nearer, the girl glanced up. She looked very surprised to see Rosie, and scrambled to her feet, scooping her cats up into her arms.

Now that she was closer, Rosie could see that the little princess's long black hair was intricately braided, and each plait was sealed with blue and gold beads. Like Rosie, the princess had gold bands around her wrists and ankles, but they were studded with blue gems. Her dark eyes were outlined with black, and the lids were covered with glittery green eye-shadow.

The girl stepped forward. "I am Princess Aisha, daughter of Pharaoh Amenophis, and I welcome you to Egypt!" she said grandly. "But how did you get here?" she added curiously.

"I'm Rosie," Rosie replied, as the cats stared at her. The ginger one had brilliant emerald-green eyes while the black cat's shone like yellow topaz. "I came by magic!" she explained.

Princess Aisha looked very excited. "Magic!" she cried. "Of course! I asked the gods for help, and they've sent *you*!"

"I hope I can help," Rosie said sympathetically. "But I don't think I was sent by the gods. What's wrong?"

Princess Aisha's face fell. "Oh, Rosie, my oldest sister, Nafretiri, is very ill!" she explained in a trembling voice. "She has had a terrible fever for the past five days, and the priests say it is caused by an evil spirit trying to take Nafretiri to the Underworld before her time."

Rosie looked puzzled. "The Underworld?"

Aisha nodded. "Where the dead go," she whispered.

"That's terrible!" Rosie gasped. "Can't anyone make Nafretiri better?"

"My father has sent for Akori, the greatest magician in Egypt," Aisha went on. "He's with Nafretiri now, and very soon he'll tell us if she can be saved." She gave a deep sigh. "I came to our beloved River Nile to make a wish and ask the gods to save my sister and everyone in Egypt." She looked hopefully at Rosie. "And then you appeared!"

"I'll do whatever I can to help," Rosie told Aisha.

Read the rest of *The Desert Princess* to follow Rosie's adventures!